Janet Hissey
Jolly Tall

SCRIBBLERS

BRAMWELL Brown was knitting a long, red scarf.

He started on Monday, knitted all Tuesday and by Wednesday it was long enough for Little Bear.

But Bramwell kept knitting.

On Thursday it fitted Little Bear and Rabbit. But still Bramwell kept knitting. By Friday it fitted Little Bear, Rabbit and Duck.

'Stop knitting!' cried Little Bear.

B<small>UT</small> Bramwell didn't stop until Saturday!

And by Sunday the scarf was too long for any of the toys.

'Why did you make it so long?' asked Little Bear.

'I just forgot to measure it,' said Bramwell.

'Never mind,' said Old Bear. 'I'm sure it will come in useful one day.'

'As a skipping rope, perhaps,' grumbled Duck.

WHILE he was skipping, Rabbit noticed a big box.
'I haven't seen that before,' he said, as he hurried over to
look. 'It might be something exciting.'

'Like treasure!' cried Little Bear.

'It's probably just a box,'
muttered Duck.

'I'LL look inside,' said Bramwell, poking a little hole with his knitting needle.

'Ouch!' said the box.

'That box just talked!' said Little Bear.

'It wasn't the box,' said Old Bear. 'It was the something inside.'

'Not treasure, then?' said Little Bear.

'Perhaps something guarding the treasure,' said Rabbit, hopefully. 'Let's open the box!'

'WE ought to talk to it first,' said Bramwell. He crept over to the little hole.

'Hello,' he called softly. 'Are you friend or foe?'

'Friend, I think,' said the voice in the box. 'I haven't heard of a foe.'

'It doesn't sound very sure,' said Duck.

'Hmmm. I'll get a net in case we have to catch it,' said Rabbit.

'I'll find a bag for the treasure,' said Little Bear.

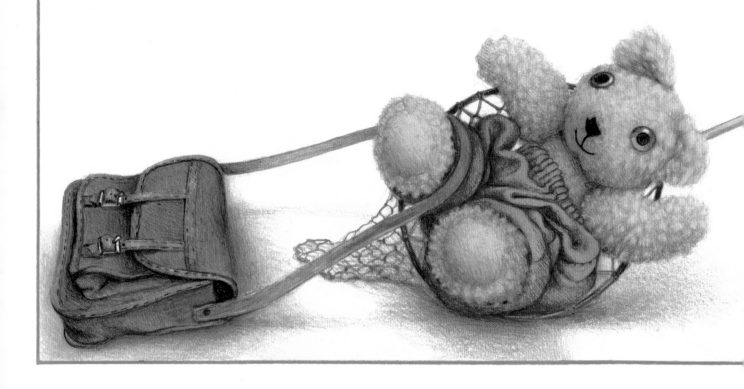

V ERY carefully, Bramwell and Old Bear
untied the string and opened the box.
Two little furry horns appeared first.
Then two big furry ears.
Then a friendly furry face.
'Hello, everyone,' it said.

'HELLO,' said Little Bear, 'are you standing on some treasure?'

'Sorry,' said their visitor. 'There's no treasure in here.'

'What are you standing on, then?' asked Rabbit.

'Just the bottom of the box,' said the smiley face.

'You must be jolly tall!' gasped Little Bear.

'That's right,' said the visitor. 'That's my name. But do call me Jolly. Do you like my house?'

'We thought it was just a box,' said Little Bear. 'It would look better with a door and some windows.'

JOLLY agreed, so they carefully cut out windows and a big front door. Bramwell made curtains to hang inside.

'You can come out now,' said Little Bear, opening the door.

'I'm afraid I can't,' said Jolly. 'I'm much too tall.'

'OH dear,' said Rabbit, 'you'll have to jump out.'

Little Bear ran out of the box. 'Look out!' he cried, as Jolly started jumping:

thump,

thump,

thump.

'It's no good,' he said, 'I just can't get high enough.'

'Don't worry,' said Old Bear. 'We'll lift you out with the crane.'

They pulled the little crane onto a pile of books.

'We'll soon have you up in the air!' called Bramwell.

'I DON'T like being high up,' said Jolly, 'I'll just stay here.'

'It's alright,' said Little Bear, 'I'll cover your eyes with my paws so you can't see how high you are.'

Jolly liked this idea so, when they were ready, Bramwell turned the handle of the crane. With Little Bear covering Jolly's eyes, they rose up out of the box.

'We're out!' cried Little Bear, taking one paw off to wave to the others.

THEN it happened . . .
Jolly saw how high he was. 'Get me down!' he cried.
  The box wobbled, Jolly wobbled and both went crashing
to the floor.

LITTLE Bear flew through the air and disappeared. But nobody noticed; they were too busy pulling Jolly out of his box.

THEY helped the wobbly Jolly to his feet again.

'Where's Little Bear?' they asked, peering into the battered box.

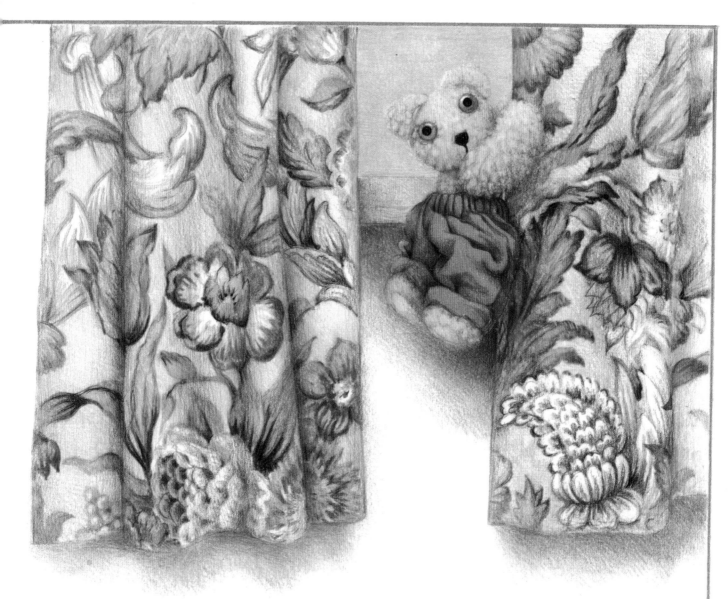

'I'M here,' came a little voice. 'I flew!'

And there was Little Bear clinging to the curtain by the tips of his paws.

'Hold on,' cried Jolly, galloping to the rescue. 'I'll get you down. Just slide down my neck.'

LITTLE Bear let go of the curtain, slid down Jolly's long neck and landed, plop, in Bramwell's net.

'That was fun,' said Little Bear. 'I want another go.'

'No more flying,' said Old Bear. 'It's time for bed.'

'But where will Jolly sleep?' asked Rabbit.

'It's alright,' said Jolly, 'giraffes sleep standing up. Just a blanket will do for me.'

LITTLE Bear and Rabbit found a cosy blanket for
their new friend.

'Your neck's going to get cold,' said
Little Bear, 'the blanket won't cover it.'

'Ah!' said Bramwell, 'I have
something for Jolly.'

He hurried away and returned with
a parcel.

'It's a present for you,' he
said. 'A welcome present!'

JOLLY unwrapped the parcel. Inside was the very, very long red scarf.

'It's the best present ever,' said Jolly. 'How did you know it would fit?'

'I guessed it would,' laughed Bramwell, as he wound it round and round Jolly's long neck.

'We thought you might be some treasure this morning,' said Rabbit.

'Or just an empty box,' said Duck.

'But we're glad you weren't,' said Little Bear. 'A new friend is better than a whole boxful of treasure!'

For Harriet and Russ

S A L A R I Y A

www.salariya.com

This edition published in Great Britain in MMXIII by Scribblers, a division of Book House,
an imprint of The Salariya Book Company Ltd
25 Marlborough Place,
Brighton BN1 1UB

www.scribblersbooks.com
www.janehissey.co.uk

First published in Great Britain in MCMXC by Hutchinson Children's Books

ISBN-13: 978-1-908973-01-6

1 3 5 7 9 8 6 4 2

A CIP catalogue record for this book is available from the British Library.

Printed and bound in China
Printed on paper from sustainable sources